Noel

USA TODAY bestselling author
H.M. Shander

Debbie
it was lovely meeting you! ♥
Shander

Noel
Published by H.M. Shander
Copyright 2020 H.M. Shander

Noel is a work of fiction. Names, characters, places, and incidents either are the products of the author's imagination or are used factitiously. Any resemblances to actual persons, living or dead, events or locals, are entirely coincidental.

Cover Design: Get Covers
Editing: PWA & IDIM Editorial
Shander, H.M., 1975—Noel

Other Reads

Run Away Charlotte
Ask Me Again
Duly Noted
That Summer
If You Say Yes
Serving Up Innocence
Serving Up Devotion
Serving Up Secrecy
Serving Up Hope
It All Began with a Note
It All Began with a Mai-Tai
It All Began with a Wedding
Whistler's Night
Return to Cheshire Bay
Adrift in Cheshire Bay
Awake in Cheshire Bay
Christmas in Cheshire Bay
Journey to Cheshire Bay

See www.hmshander.com for the complete list

Table of Contents

One

"Yes, absolutely sir. You have my word and can count on me." I hung up the phone and stared at it, shaking my head in disbelief.

My executive assistant job description within the world of Holden Enterprises just added a new '*other jobs as required*' item to my ever-growing bullet list. Now I had to go and pick up the CEO's fowl-mouthed ten-year-old from school and drive him home as his mother was sitting in the emergency room with pelvic pains. Of course, Daniel Holden was rushing to his wife's side; there wasn't anything he wouldn't do for her, except tell her it was over, and run away with me.

I rose from my plush leather chair and sauntered over to my secretary, with my clutch tucked under my arm. "Janice, I'll be gone for the rest of the afternoon. Forward all calls to voice mail, and I'll check on them later."

"Sure thing, Ms. Edwards." The lady, old enough to pass for my mother, started rustling the scattered papers on her desk. "Anything else I can do for you?"

"Yes, actually, there is one more thing." I paused and worked through my thoughts to make sure it was attainable. "When your work is done, you can take the rest of the afternoon off."

"What?" She tipped her head to the side as if she didn't hear me.

"You can leave early." I tugged down my blazer as I smiled at Janice. She was one of the hardest working employees I had and deserved a break. "Maybe go shopping for your darling grandbaby."

"Thank you, Ms. Edwards. Shall I text you when I leave?"

"No need. As long as your work is done, that's all that matters. Just make sure the Fuentes account is caught up and sitting on my desk."

"Yes, ma'am." She beamed. "Thank you so much."

It was nearly Christmas. Everyone deserved a break. "Great, see you Monday. Enjoy your weekend."

I didn't hang around to hear her gush on and on, something she did non-stop when I gave her a bit of unexpected, yet paid, time off, or gave her a lavish gift. Janice was always so grateful, but her gratitude was almost too sweet. A simple thank you was enough.

I stepped into the elevator and pushed the parkade level - plus side of running personal errands for Daniel was the use of his Audi.

I pressed the button on the remote and the car beeped, flashing its headlights. Slipping inside, I snuggled into the rich interior, scented in his expensive and exotic cologne, and started the vehicle. It was much louder than my Tesla and the rattling caught me off guard. It had been a while since I'd been in Daniel's vehicle, and it definitely wasn't being driven the last time I was. Brushing away the thought of riding him, I gave the school address to the GPS and it plotted it out nicely. Thirty-minutes away. Perfect. Lots of time for me to belt out my favourite Christmas carols.

As predicted, I pulled up thirty minutes flat in front of the school in the kiss and go section. School wasn't out for another hour, so it wasn't like I was taking up space needed for the nannies in the minivans or the school buses. Did kids at an exclusive prep school even take the yellow bus, or were they all chauffeured? Regardless, I wasn't going to be here long enough for it to matter.

I armed the red sedan, and shoulders back, walked to the main door and buzzed.

"Yes?" A voice crackled over the intercom.

"Britannia Edwards. I'm here to pick up Bentley Waltham."

Why they chose to give their child a different last name was something I never understood. Daniel and the missus had been photographed with their kid at several high-profile events. Maybe if he was never in the spotlight, it would make sense. But that was on them, and it wasn't my concern, although I wasn't going to deny the curiosity.

"Come in."

The door clicked and I pulled it open, stepping into the foyer where it looked like Christmas threw up. Ornaments, clearly decorated by the students, hung from every imaginable surface. A giant tree with full boxes of mittens and toques and toiletries sat off to the side and a symphony of choral music floated down the hall.

I turned and walked into the office.

"Merry Christmas." The receptionist was dressed in one of those ugly sweaters and sported a set of angel wings.

"Yes, Merry Christmas." My voice matched hers in melody. It was my favourite time of year, one I could celebrate 365 days if possible. "Bentley Waltham, please."

"Sure, sure. He's in room 114, just down the hall. When you've collected his things, just bring him back here, lovey, and we'll sign him out."

I nodded and walked out, passing Christmas overload as I tried my best to not click down the hallways in my SJPs.

Painted pictures of candles decorated one wall, and clothespin angels hung from the ceiling, making it look like the entrance surrounding

Heaven or something. Everywhere I went, I was greeted with more and more Christmas and seeing it all, put a little spring in my step. Bing Crosby even sang in the speakers overhead.

At the entrance to room 114, I paused. A male with a deep baritone was reading a story, the inflections pitching and falling as he changed voices. It was enchanting, and I didn't want to interrupt his charming storytelling.

After a moment, however, a child spoke. "Mr. S. Someone's at the door."

"Oh?" The squeaking of his runners across the floor grew in strength.

A man – a gorgeous man with the perfect amount of scruff – appeared in my field of view. He was taller than Daniel, at least six feet tall, with a slender build. Dressed in an ugly sweater vest and sporting reindeer antlers, he stopped at the entrance.

I didn't miss the way he gazed at me. "Can I help you?"

"Sorry to interrupt. I'm here to pick up Bentley."

"Oh? Usually I meet Mrs. Holden outside."

Good, he was sceptical, as he should be,

Daniel would be pleased to know it.

"I know, and I apologize for the last minute change in plans. Mr. Holden sent me to pick him up as Mrs. Holden," I leaned in closer. "She's having a bit of an emergency."

"Oh dear." His dark brown eyes connected with me and held me there. It was hard to break free. "Are you on Bentley's approved pick up list?"

"Possibly?" I shrugged since I honestly had no idea.

"Well, let's find out. These kids are precious to me and…"

"I understand completely, and I'm grateful you're taking the precautions necessary."

He turned back into his class. "Mrs. B, I'll be right back. Can you finish up?" The handsome teacher pointed into the hallway. "Let's head back to the office."

"Sure thing."

"And you are?" He cocked a brow.

"My apologies, Britannia Edwards." I thrust out my hand as if I was in a board meeting. "I'm Daniel Holden's assistant."

Once again, he took more than a few heartbeats to scan me up and down and methodically all the way back up, settling on my face. "I see."

As we walked down the hall, a jingle of bells came from Mr. S, and I searched until I found the source. On the reindeer ears, as decorations, were several tiny bells. "Your headwear is cute."

"Oh, yeah, can't help myself. Christmas is my favourite holiday." He pulled it off and gripped the headband in his hand. "Besides the kids love it."

"You're a good story-teller, by the way. I wish my grade-school teachers were as enchanting."

"A little dry, were they?"

"Let's just say, my schooling wasn't as nice as these kids. My school never looked like this." I pointed to the floating angels as we walked by.

"Maybe you just don't remember it?"

"I remember everything."

Every. Single. Thing.

Probably helped me scale the corporate ladder within the two companies I'd last worked for before joining Daniel's. I was the kind of person who only had to be told something once, and it was committed to memory.

"Really?" There was a hint of a sparkle in his eyes. "Are you a fan of the season?"

"Are you asking me if I'm a Grinch? The answer is no. I just don't go all out and immerse myself in it the way some people do it." There was a decorated tree in my apartment and a mini one in my office. That was all I needed.

"So… Christmas lights hanging in your vehicle would be a hard no?"

I laughed, until I saw the seriousness on his chiselled face. Did he have them in his? That would be a sight to see.

He waltzed into the office. "Can you pull Bentley's file and see if Mrs. Edwards is on it?"

"Miss. It's Miss Edwards." Stunned by own admission, I bit my lip. What was happening to me? I inhaled and brought forth my best boardroom face, but not the one I gave to Daniel.

"Nice. *Miss* Edwards." His gaze lingered on me for a couple of steely breaths before turning to the computer screen in front of the secretary.

"She's on there." A no-nonsense voice projected from the other side of a wall, before he moved into sight. "Hi. Christian Teige, I'm the

9

principal here." Danny DeVito's cousin stood approvingly, making me feel much taller than my five-foot five height.

The principal faced the secretary. "Mr. Holden called here three-quarters of an hour ago. She's already been cleared."

"Great. Let's get Bentley packed up." Mr. S rolled himself up to his full size. "Shall we, Miss?" He positioned the antlers back on his head. Stunning without them, now Mr. S looked even more adorable.

"Yes, of course."

A mild sense of dejavu tickled at me as I walked the length of hall again.

"Have you been working for Mr. Holden's company for a while?" There was a smug smile on his face and that twinkle in his eye returned in full force. "This is the first time I've seen you around."

Ah, did Mr. Holden's reputation for dismissing his assistants quickly proceed him?

"I'm his *executive* assistant, so yes." I added for good measure. I had to work hard in the corporate world to level up, and although my job came with a side of good timing, as I transferred in from another company, I still had to bust my ass.

Time off was a luxury I didn't have, and even being in this school for ten minutes, my phone was vibrating enough to have the potential to be pleasurable.

Of course, I was sure there was gossip on the top floor about the particular ladder I was climbing, but Daniel was different. Our Monday morning power meetings always ended breathlessly, and he promised things with Mrs. Holden were over, and by the new year we'd be able to start being together. Finally.

"Six months."

"You've been there six months?"

Searing heat crossed my chest, and I was glad I'd dressed modestly. "No, I meant, two years." I turned my focus to the door we stood in front of. What a horrible faux-pas to have slipped out - six months had been how long I'd been secretly banging the boss.

"Those are different time frames."

"Yes." I cleared my throat. "Can I take Bentley now?"

"Of course." Mr. S walked into class and gently whispered to the child.

I'd only met Bentley a handful of times,

and each time, the little jackass rubbed me the wrong way. It could've been his holier than thou view.

"Hey, lady." The entitled brat stopped in front of me and slowly raked his gaze over me, a wicked familiar smile forming. "You're looking fine."

He was also a miniature version of his father, which was probably part of the reason I didn't like him. It was weird for a kid to talk to a grown up the way he did, as well as stare at me like I was a piece of meat. I was old enough to be his mother. The very thought made me shudder.

"Bentley." I looked down my nose while greeting him.

"Why are you here?"

"Your father asked me to pick you up."

He snorted and pitched a few of his personal effects onto the floor. "You got the wrong time. School's not done."

"I know." It's not like I could blurt out about his mother having some sort of emergency. "Your father has an adventure planned for you." I connected with Bentley's teacher. It was kind of an adventure, right? Depending on how things were with the missus, they could be back and forth to the hospital, but judging by the look on Mr. S's face, I was out of my league with kids.

He picked up the tossed backpack and held it for Bentley. "Your dad has an important meeting with just you." He tapped the tip of his nose.

"So why doesn't he pick me up?"

"Because this is part of his plan." He rose to his full height.

The kid's expression said it all. Yeah, I wasn't buying the teacher's story either. At least mine sounded fun. Meetings weren't for kids, even I knew that.

"Whatever." Bentley threw his backpack over his shoulders. "Probably fired the nanny again and that's why she's here." A stiff thumb pointed in my direction, talking about me rather than to me.

It gave me pause, though. Did Daniel go through house staff as quickly as office staff?

"I'm sure there's a good reason for Miss Edwards being your ride home today, Mr. Bentley. Part of the magic of the season. Sometimes you just have to believe in the goodness."

I stifled my laugh. Yeah, that wasn't it. I was the only one available to take the brat home.

13

There was no magic involved at all.

"Remember, Christmas Concert on Monday. Wear your best outfit."

Bentley started to walk away, but I stopped and faced the teacher. "By the way, what's your name?"

"Noel Sullivan." He extended his hand, to which I held and gave my best power shake. "You should really try to attend the concert. It's really adorable and not to be missed. It's here on Monday evening, starts at six."

Kids weren't my thing, but the charming way Noel smiled was melting the icicles around the thought. "Perhaps I will, Mr. Sullivan."

I waved and sauntered away, adding an extra little bounce as I did. Shameless? Sure. However, it was intoxicating to have someone check me out who wasn't part of Holden Enterprises.

Two

I straddled the chair which held the CEO and gazed into his heady eyes. As I bent down to kiss his lips, he twisted his head away.

"Sorry." Taken by the moment, I'd forgotten Daniel's rule – no kissing on the lips. It was too personal. Because you know, banging your assistant in the board room hardly qualified as personal.

I inched my way off and tugged down my skirt. "Are you going to the concert tonight?"

All weekend long, for the oddest reason, my thoughts revolved around the possibility of seeing Noel in his cute reindeer antlers.

"What concert?"

"Bentley's. At the school."

"I never go to those."

"Never?"

After disposing of the double condom, he pulled his dress pants on and buttoned his shirt. Always preferring to not get anything wrinkled, he laid everything neatly on the back of one of the boardroom chairs before he got down to business.

"I don't have time for that nonsense."

Not that I should've found that surprising, considering how often he was in the office, but still, wasn't family supposed to come first? The missus always did.

"How's your wife doing?"

He glared, probably because I had accidentally placed an emphasis on the wife part. At least I said *your* when I very well could've said *the.* I was still waiting for her to be the ex, so we could explore a deeper relationship beyond the boardroom.

"Ectopic pregnancy. They cut out her tube Friday night but she's home resting."

"Oh, I'm sorry. I had no idea she was pregnant."

"Me either." It was said so harshly I instantly wondered if the missus was having an affair, not that Daniel had a right to be angry since he was doing the very thing. With me. And maybe a couple of others. Who knew?

"Are you going to tell her about us yet?"

He tugged his suit jacket on, and I reached out to straighten his tie.

"Oh, for sure. In the new year. Right now, this isn't a good time, especially after the pregnancy loss."

My heart cracked a little. "I suppose I could wait a couple more weeks, but I need to know this is going somewhere. I can't be just your play toy."

"Play toy?" He cupped the side of my cheek. "Is that how you think I see you?"

I buttoned my blouse and pulled my wavy hair out from under the collar. "It's just you've been saying for weeks now how you two are over, and I keep wondering when I'll get you all to myself? And not just in this boardroom."

"Soon, okay?" He kissed my forehead. "You ready?"

I wasn't and turned to check out my reflection on the stainless-steel water pitcher. We had another rule for our power meetings, no touching of my hair. This way, it wouldn't look like anything other than professional meetings went on, whether the staff believed it or not, at least there was an effort on my part. I tucked in my shirt while he rested his forearms on the chair. Giving myself a quick once over while I stepped back into my heels, I nodded. iPad secured in my arm; we were set to put on another Academy award performance.

He walked to the door and slowly cracked it open. "I'm glad we cleared that up." He carried on his charade as we moved out into the hall. "Get on the phone and tell Marty we're not bending."

"I'm on it, Mr. Holden." I tapped a finger on the locked screen.

Daniel stopped in front of his secretary; a young thing I'd give a month of working here before she was canned. She wasn't as kiss-ass as the others had been. "Nevaeh, can you reschedule lunch services for an hour earlier? This meeting went long, and I'm getting hungry." He looked at me as if it was my fault it took him too long to get going.

"Sure thing."

Yep, she forgot to add the *sir.* I'd give her 'til the new year.

He drummed his stubby fingers on the desk. "Next Monday, block out two hours for the boardroom, and we'll need to have breakfast served at the start. Go with fruit and bagels, and Earl Grey."

My favourite tea, how sweet he remembered.

Nevaeh glanced at her keyboard. "It's Christmas Eve."

"Exactly. I'll need to make sure everything is covered for the holidays." He cocked an eyebrow in such a way my panties would've melted off, had I still had them on. "Miss Edwards, I expect you to be in attendance."

"Of course. I'll put it into my schedule."

"Great. And I expect the updated report before noon." Another scene in his charade, but it worked. Neveah seemed totally unsuspecting.

I turned and strode away as fast as possible to my office and locked the door upon entering. In the bottom drawer, I pulled out a package of feminine hygiene wipes and a new black lace thong, and set to cleaning myself up. After that was done, I sat at my desk and scheduled the two-hour boardroom meeting for Christmas Eve, setting a reminder in my phone to wear the green and gold garter belt and matching panties for him. I'd give him a Christmas Eve he won't soon forget. Pushing away the multiple positions I had planned, I dug into my work.

Janice knocked quietly on my door. "I'm leaving in a few minutes. Is there anything you'd like before I go?"

"I'm good, thanks. Enjoy your lunch."

She chuckled as her whole body shook. "It's nearly five, ma'am."

"Seriously?"

How had I lost track of the day like that? I'd been so engrossed on the one account I hadn't noticed the sky outside my office window had darkened, and as I stretched out my ears, the general hum in the office was gone; it was eerily quiet.

I looked Janice in the eyes, apologizing with one easy glance. "Well, in that case, enjoy your evening. Just leave the door open."

"Everything okay?"

"Of course." A fake smile stretched out my painted lips.

"You've just been in here all day. You didn't even leave for lunch."

"Just trying to get ahead before the holidays."

Next week, with Christmas falling on a Tuesday, I'd given my staff a week's vacation, myself included. I planned on taking at least two of those days actually off – not even remotely working – but I needed to make sure everything was ready for me to do just that.

"If you're sure?"

I stopped typing and smiled. "Honestly, I'm good. Thanks for letting me know how late it was." I saved my progress. "Actually, I should probably get going myself. I have an appointment at six."

Daniel said it was a waste of time, but I was looking forward to seeing the kiddie concert, but if I were being truthful with myself, it was Mr. Sullivan I was most interested in watching. With a thirty-minute drive ahead of me, I barely had time to stop and grab a bite.

"Have a good night, Ms. Edwards." She backed out, and I listened as she slammed her drawer and locked it up. The jingle of her keys faded as she moved towards the elevator.

I pulled out a backup make-up kit and set it on my desk, folding open the mirror. Quickly I ran a comb through my perfectly coloured hair and spritzed it with hair shine. Confident in how nicely my curls bounced, I ran a brushing of powder over my t-zone and dabbed on a darker shade of plum across my lips, giving a quick pout. All in order, I popped a mint in my mouth and tucked everything back into my drawer. On the back of my door, I kept a couple of extra outfits, but everything screamed business. A glance to the clock told me there wasn't enough time to run home and throw on a pair of jeans. However, I quickly set a reminder to make sure to bring more casual clothes to work.

Ten minutes later, I locked my office and headed to Bentley's school, curious to see this concert, but more than intrigued to see his teacher again.

Parking was a nightmare. I ended up leaving my Tesla blocks away and by time I made my way into the entrance, I was frozen to the bone. Since I hadn't imagined the parking situation to be so horrible, I was ill prepared in heels, bare legs, and an overcoat. I stepped into the warmth of the foyer with a grand sigh, and stood off to the side shaking, allowing the warmth to permeate my pores.

"Hey, if it isn't Miss Edwards."

A broad smile immediately perked up my cheeks when I spotted Bentley's teacher walking toward me in suit. It upped him from charmingly cute to downright handsome. He'd fit in well as a poster child of Holden Enterprises.

"If it isn't Mr. S."

"You actually came?" He stepped close enough a hint of freshly applied – albeit cheaper than Holden's – cologne tickled my nose.

"Why do you sound so surprised? You said it wasn't to be missed."

He tipped his head down. "Perhaps I did."

An involuntary shudder coursed through my body.

"You cold?"

"Freezing. I had no idea about the parking."

"Yeah, with a thousand students, it becomes a logistical nightmare. We had parents lining up at four."

"Seriously? Why would anyone line up two hours before a children's concert?" It was beyond comprehensible to me.

"For the best seats. We don't have reserved seating."

It was a school and not the symphony. I nodded, even if I didn't understand.

"Is Bentley with you?"

A small smirk teased my lips, and I tipped my head toward him. "Did you see him with me?"

"He hasn't arrived yet. I was just out looking for him when I spotted you, figured you'd brought him."

"Oh." My smirk fell. "I know Daniel, um, Mr. Holden, said he had plans. Maybe that included Bentley?"

"Too bad. That boy was part of my tenor section." He waved at a few parents as they stomped their way into the entrance and shook out their coats. "Are you still going to stay if he's not here?"

I leaned closer to Noel and whispered.

"How weird would it be if I did?"

I had no other connection to the school, and Bentley was a pretty loose connection at that.

"Do you just want to hang out with me then or would you rather fight the crowds for a seat?"

I glanced around and shrugged at the mass of people. "I'd rather hang out with you, since you're the only one I know, if the Holdens aren't here. Besides, I'll have a much better view of the show, right?"

What could possibly be worse than that?

Three

For someone who had had little to no experience with children, the concert was a genuine hoot. Most definitely, it was the younger kids who stole the show with their precociousness and innocence, but the older kids certainly closed out the performance with a haunting rendition of *O Holy Night,* enough to cause goosebumps from head to toe.

I rose from my seat on the side of the auditorium and hung back, watching as Noel interacted with the parents and hugged a few of the children. The concert was two hours long, and my phone had buzzed incessantly throughout. While waiting for the teacher, I flipped through my texts, nothing of importance, or at least nothing that warranted my immediate attention. My heart sped up though when I spotted a text from Daniel and clicked to open it. There he was, spread-eagled at his desk, naked as a jaybird, grinning from ear to ear. It was hard to focus on his face with everything else in plain sight.

Quickly, I tapped back out of the messages. That was meant for my eyes only, likely his *wife* probably didn't even see that much, and definitely not a room full of parents and children. However, the image had imprinted on my brain, and my body responded, warming nicely, complete with a fresh set of tingles and a deep ache forming between my legs.

A week was a long time to wait. And a couple more weeks of waiting lay ahead of me until he told his wife he was leaving.

As Noel walked over, I pocketed my phone. "Still working?"

"It never ends." But I smiled as I said it. I knew what I was getting into when I started down this path - a life with luxuries, and also a hefty price tag and a few sacrifices, but it was worth it.

Noel was beaming, grandeur than Daniel's

playful smile still burned onto the back of my retinas. "What did you think of the concert?"

"Honestly, I loved it. It was really cute."

"Didn't the kids do a great job?" He waved to a family. "I'm so proud of all of them." There was so much pride oozing from his lips it was hard to not be affected by it.

"That's really sweet. You like your job, don't you?"

"My mom always said, do something you love, and you'll never have to work a day in your life. And she was right."

I laughed, as it was so different than my upbringing. "I was told to dream big and work my ass off to achieve it, and don't let anyone tell you no."

"And how's that going for you?"

"Pretty well. I certainly can't complain."

"That's great." He nodded but looked over my shoulder, stepping off to the side but quickly tapping my arm. "I have a few things left to do, but can I interest you in a coffee afterwards?"

"I don't drink coffee, but sure, I have time for a quick drink."

"Give me five?"

"Of course."

I wasn't sure why I agreed so easily to Noel's request. Going for coffee, as the expression goes, wasn't going to get me anywhere. Not really. But there was something about this guy pulling me in. He was so different than Daniel. Never once had I heard Daniel express pride in his staff doing a job well done, in fact, I didn't even warrant that kind of compliment after our private power meetings. I never got a thank you, or anything. Hmm...Not even after a *job* well done. Like this morning.

"Penny for your thoughts?"

"What? Sorry. Was just thinking about this morning's board meeting." I blinked away the images of Daniel, the sensation of his touch, and the heady scent of sex as it hung in the air.

"Must've been some meeting." He stared into my eyes, and I focused on the man before me.

"Yeah, it was." My voice softened as I pushed away naughty work thoughts. "So, where's a good place to *grab a coffee?*"

"Are you familiar with this part of town?"

I shook my head. My apartment was near the office, and I passed the turnoff to it on my way here. "I have Google maps though, so I can find anything."

"There's this indie coffee place on 12th and Jackson called *Chai One On.* They make a mean hot chocolate."

"How mean?" I found myself leaning closer to him.

"Spicy mean."

"A spicy hot chocolate? This I have to try."

A family approached him trying not to be subtle at all in wanting to speak to Noel.

"Meet you there?" Let him chat with his parents. They were important.

"Sure."

I walked away, but kept turning back to see him, and each time, he was watching me. It made my heart skip a beat.

* * *

I grabbed a bistro table for two in the coffeeshop and thumbed through my messages. Another from Daniel. This time he was holding a firm version of himself. Just seeing it caused heat to flood into my cheeks. I really needed to look at this more in depth when I got home.

"Hey." Noel's voice rang out as he snuck

over towards me.

"Hey." I quickly flipped my phone over and pushed the off button.

"Didn't mean to interrupt."

"It was just my boss."

Noel's gaze fell to my phone in such a way I just knew he'd seen the photo and there was no way to deny it. "Your boss. Got it."

Seventy-three scenarios played through my mind, and none of them were attractive. Saying the word *friend* would have given it a different connotation, but because the truth had always rolled out of me first, it was the word boss. Now, I was positive the reason why Noel hung back a little further was because I was a corporate ladder climber, but for all the wrong ways. He likely figured I was sleeping my way to the top, which couldn't be further from the truth. I busted my lady-balls to get where I was - Daniel was just a perk with a promise.

Finally, after a few moments of silence passed, he cleared his throat. "Interested in trying that hot chocolate?"

"I'd love to, thank you."

Noel walked over to the counter where a

friendly barista touched his hand, smiled sheepishly, and blushed as he gave his order. Her gaze floated around the space when he ordered two hot chocolate supremes and landed on me, morphing her expression. Judging by the drastic change in temperament, I was going to get a spitball in mine.

He returned and sat across from me, leaning back in his chair.

"You come here a lot, eh?"

"Often enough. Can I be frank?"

"I thought you were Noel?" I laughed at my own joke, which didn't seem to have the same effect on him.

"Do you believe in the spirit of Christmas?"

"As in, it's better to give than to receive?" Because I was all over that. I loved spoiling my staff with lavish and practical gifts.

"More than that." He uncrossed his legs and put both feet on the floor, leaning his forearms on the table. "The magic of the season."

"I'm not following you."

He assessed me, probably came with the job of herding children – the ability to see if the person was lying or telling the truth. "Do you think things happen for a reason, or do you think it's blind luck when something good happens?"

"Honestly, I believe that if you work hard, good things happen as a result."

He studied me again, his brows knitting together in deep thought. "So… no magic is involved?"

I shook my head. "Never."

"And everything happens for a reason?"

"Always."

"Hmm…" He leaned back when the young barista set down our large cups, with a mound of whip cream and brown powder sprinkled overtop. "Thank you." He pushed one my way. "Try it."

Hesitantly I lifted the heavy mug laden with more calories than I burned in HIIT class to my lips, and slowly tipped it back until the heat of the liquid damn near scalded the tip of my tongue. However, it was tasty, and there was a definite spice lingering.

"It's good." I set it down, licking off the remnants of whipped cream.

"My favourite treat." He took a gentle sip and set his mug back onto the saucer. "So back to you."

"Why back to me?"

"Because we're out on a date, and I'm-"

"Whoa, buddy. When did this turn out to be a date?" I pushed back in my chair, putting some much-needed distance between us.

"When I asked, and you said yes." There was confidence in his voice, and the casual way he responded, it was mildly intriguing.

I narrowed my eyes in a playful gesture and added a sly smile. "I hardly thought it was a date. More of a get together."

It had been so long since I'd been with a member of the opposite sex outside a boardroom, but this hardly qualified as a date. Dates involved cheesy lines, flowers and poetry, and usually a hint of awkwardness.

He mirrored my grin. "You are aware of how dates work, right? A guy asks a girl, and they go do something together."

"That's a pretty loose interpretation of the word date."

"Unless, of course, you are seeing someone that would object to us being here together?" His gaze fell to the phone still face down.

Four

I didn't even know how to answer his question. Daniel and I were complicated. There wasn't anything I wouldn't do for the guy, and he knew it. I loved him, which he also knew. But beyond boardroom A, we were boss and assistant, nothing more, no matter how much I wanted him outside those walls. My time was coming, however. Just a few more weeks.

"Well…"

Noel huffed and stretched out. "It's not my place. Forget I asked."

"Why did you ask?"

"Because I'm interested in getting to know

you better. That's what dates are all about. You take someone out, try them on for size and go from there. Haven't you been on a date before?"

"Several times," I stammered out, but I racked my brain as to when the last one actually was.

There was that guy in university, but that was years ago. What? Really? Years ago? As I sat there and remembered, it had in fact been a very long time. Once I started working in the corporate world, the dating just fell the wayside as it wasn't a priority. Holy smokes. How could that have gone on for as long as it had? Thank goodness for Daniel, to break me from my rut and lavish a little attention on me and my lady bits.

"What about you? You date all the time?" I asked it in jest.

Noel ran his fingers through his hair. "Actually, yeah. But I just haven't found that one person I'd want to see after a coffee."

"Why do I find that so hard to believe?" Noel was a sweetheart with above average looks. He had a heart of gold who clearly doted on his students.

"I don't know. Why do you?" He took a

long, lingering sip of his hot chocolate.

"Because it's not believable. My intuition tells me."

"Do you always listen to your gut?"

"It's never steered me wrong before." Not once. I trusted it.

"So why the delay in answering if you have someone waiting for you back home?"

"For starters, you never asked that. You asked if I was seeing someone, and—"

"Yet, you never really answered."

I twirled my cup on the saucer, warring within myself how to answer. "Fine, there is someone I'm seeing."

Someone I saw every single day. Someone who rewarded my hard work with a little Monday morning perk me up. Someone who someday was going to leave his wife, pick me and together we'd run away forever.

"Fantastic. I'm glad we got that all cleared up."

If he was so glad, then why did I suddenly feel like I'd been kicked in the gut? In the span of a few minutes, I'd revealed more about myself than I had to anyone, and I really hadn't said much.

Putting some space between us, he leaned back in his bistro chair and propped his foot on his knee. "How's your hot chocolate?"

"It's good, thanks."

But I couldn't bring myself to taste anymore. A lump had formed in the back of my throat, my brain blanked out completely and I had no idea what to do now. Clearly, this date, get together, or whatever, did not go the way he had hoped, and now he sat there with a droopy expression. Did I leave? Did I finish up my drink? Did I wait to see if he'd leave first and then follow him out? I was in uncharted territory and completely lost, something I didn't like feeling.

Noel set down an empty mug, its hollowness ringing out as it scraped against the saucer. "Sorry if I struck a nerve. That wasn't my intention."

"What was your intention?"

He shrugged. "I don't know, really. I just don't want to spend time getting to know someone if it won't be reciprocated. Been there, done that, and wrote the book on the rejection."

"I'm sorry. Romance isn't easy." My own success stories were zero. I was still trying to win the heart of my boss.

"Who said anything about romance?" A weak grin pushed out on the left side of his face. "So, since you're seeing this guy," he tapped my phone, "I guess this will be the last time we see each other?"

"You give up that easily?" I cocked my recently manicured eyebrow. The idea of being hunted was a mild turn on, and who wouldn't enjoy being preyed on once in a while?

"No sense fishing for something I have no hope in catching. Not interested in catch and release."

"But what about the thrill of the chase? Isn't that what all guys enjoyed?"

Daniel had mentioned several times over how he loved going to war on various businesses, and when they finally signed the merger or his takeover, he always found it anticlimactic because the hunt was done. He enjoyed beating the company down until they accepted his proposal. The signings were merely a formality.

"Don't get me wrong, I enjoy the thrill of it all, but I have to be able to see the end goal."

"As in marriage right off the bat?" Dating's

end goal was walking down the aisle, right?

"As in commitment. Someone I want to take to Christmas parties and show off. Someone I can call when I'm having a bad day who'll cheer me up or just let me vent. Someone special I can share all my joys with."

"Ah," I said, taking a long sip of the cooling drink. "You want the fantasy."

"Don't you?"

Under the weight of his stare, I broke our eye contact. I already had the fantasy, sort of. Where Daniel was the quintessential man; a bold and shrewd businessman, cover-worthy stud, and an utter delight in the sex department, he was kind of a dud in the conversational part. And never once had he treated me to a hot chocolate or anything that was his favourite. As for venting? Never did it, except business wise, and he never listened to me. Never tried to cheer me up either. Wow… based on Noel's criteria, Daniel wouldn't measure very high.

Noel's chair scraped across the tile floor, breaking my thoughts in half. "Well, Britannia, it's been interesting."

"Wait, that's it?" I rose from my chair as

well. "You're not even going to ask for my number?"

A part of me had been willing to give it out too, to see if there was more to Noel than there was to Daniel, and right now, the deck was stacked slightly more toward Noel, despite the brush off. It was nice having a conversation that didn't involve mergers, acquisitions, and business.

"Is there any point? You've already said you're spoken for."

"Not in those words." Why was I getting so upset over him leaving? I put my overcoat on.

"Seriously, it's all good. That's why I suggested coffee, and not dinner. It's easier to end it if things aren't going well, or if the lady fesses up her heart belongs to another." Elegantly, he slipped into his thick, woolly jean jacket. "Thanks for meeting me and thanks for attending the concert. Give my regards to Bentley when you see him next."

With that, he set his dirty mug on the counter and strode away without a backwards glance. I didn't even get to say goodbye.

# # #

I sat at my desk, flipping through papers on an upcoming acquisition when Daniel strode into my office without a knock.

"Miss Edwards."

My hands froze between two court documents as I stared at the confident swagger walking into my space.

"New suit?" It was the first time I'd laid my eyes on him all day.

"Yes. Elizabeth picked it out for me last week when she needed some retail therapy." He threw his hands out to the side and spun around.

Had to admit, the wife had impeccable taste as the suit fit him perfectly and the dark blue was a great colour on him as it brought out the colour of his eyes. "What can I help you with?"

He wiggled his eyebrows and shut the door, engaging the lock. "Something only you can fix." With grace, he strode over my side of the desk and waited. I gathered the papers and set them in a pile off to the side, where he immediately sat. "You see, I have this ache."

Yeah, I knew exactly how to fix that. It was my speciality. "By the way, thanks for all the pictures you sent me last night. Your son's teacher happened to accidentally see one of them."

"How was that?" He tipped his head.

"I was at Bentley's concert."

"What were you doing there?"

"Watching."

"Why?"

"Because I was invited."

"By whom?"

"Mr. Sullivan."

"Are you screwing my kid's teacher?" There was more than a subtle amount of jealousy in his tone. "Thought I was enough of a man for you?" His voice changed into a sugary sweet mess as he cupped my chin.

But I didn't answer. Maybe if Daniel knew how it felt to be dangled like a carrot, he'd finally stop pretending to be in love with his wife, admit his feelings for me, and have us ride off into the sunset.

He stroked my cheek with the pad of his thumb. "Darling, you know you're all mine, and I can't share. It's just not my nature."

"But I have to share you." I tore my gaze away as he shifted across my desk; it wasn't hard to miss the growing attraction he felt for me.

"Only for a little while. You can have me now if you'd like?" His hand moved from my chin, over the shoulder of my silky tank top, and down the length of my muscley arm, with soft, touchable skin. His fingers intertwined with mine, and he kissed and sucked each of my fingertips until my core lit on fire and a heat burned so intensely, I thought I'd explode right there. It was mind-boggling how fast it flared up. "See what you do to me?"

See it? I felt the pressure beneath my hand. He was as hard as a rock.

"Why don't you help me relieve some stress?" He leaned back and unfastened his belt, followed by an unzipping of his new suit pants.

"I really should get back to finishing this. The courts need the papers by ten tomorrow morning, and with the holidays, I don't want to overlook anything and have to push back with any kind of delay."

"This won't take long, promise. I'd know you want to make me happy. I know you licking the lollipop makes you happy too, and I'd be happy to return the favour. I'm getting hungry for a little beaver snack." His voice was so sweet, and his eyes had the deepest pleading with the power to cut through my resistance.

Beaver tails were my favourite. I loved the way he kissed up the insides of my legs and twirled his tongue in just the perfect way. Resistance was futile.

"How do you want me?" I purred, an ache building between my legs.

"Oh, you can just stay like that." He unzipped all the way and leaned back, giving me the lead.

"You're not going to take them off?"

He popped his head up. "No. Just don't drool on my new pants."

I reached into the drawer where I kept a couple of flavoured bj condoms and rolled one down his impressive length.

"I really wish you'd let me go bare." His voice hitched as I wrapped my hand around him.

"And I'd really wish you'd let me kiss you."

"You're about to." His eyebrows danced as I palmed him.

"I mean your lips." I manoeuvred my chair

closer as my finger dared to trace the outline of his mouth while I dipped it into its cavity, allowing him to suck on the tips of it. God damn, it was hot. I pulled my finger out and licked it; that was as close to a kiss as I was going to get. For now.

"Sweet, baby. One day soon. I promise."

"Do you love me, Daniel?" I poised my hot, eager mouth over the coconut-flavoured latex tip, waiting for his answer.

The phone on my desk rang, and with Daniel still tightly gripped in my hand, I gave the display a passing glance. "It's Janice, but I want an answer. Do you love me?"

Unexpectedly, Daniel grunted and picked up the receiver. "Miss Edwards office."

Give credit where it was do, it was a fabulous stall technique.

"We're in the middle of something, can't it wait?" He sighed and passed me the phone. "For you."

Janice piped up. "I'm really sorry, Miss Edwards, but there's a man here to see you."

I dropped my gaze from Daniel's narrowed slits. "What? Really? Who?"

"Noel Sullivan."

Five

What was Noel doing here? Without skipping a beat, I checked out the time. It was after four. School was finished. Still didn't explain why he was here, but at least it wasn't during school hours.

"Alright, thank you, Janice. I'll be out in a minute." I put the receiver in its cradle and stared up into a dark pair of eyes boring into mine. "Your son's teacher is here."

"We're not finished." He repositioned himself, clearly the interruption had not dampened his spirits.

My own ache had disappeared with the first ring, and the aggravation rolling off Daniel wasn't

47

helping. "You tell him that. Besides, you never answered my question."

Daniel hopped off my desk and threw the condom into the wastebasket, which I covered it with a tissue when he stomped away. In haste, he tucked himself back into his pants and made himself presentable while at the same time sending me a penetrating glare. He yanked an empty file folder off the top of my filing cabinet to hide the fact the interruption hadn't killed his desire. To me, the ill placed office supply looked highly suspicious, but I had no doubt he'd be able to make it work, it was part of his charm.

He shot me a fake smile and whispered through gritted teeth. "Game on."

I rose and followed him to the door he was slowly opening. "I want an answer."

He cleared his throat and for good measure, raised his voice. "Since you have a visitor, can we finish our discussion in a few minutes?" His expression was unreadable, but I wasn't going to make it change by saying no.

I stared back.

"I'll be in my office when you're done here." He stepped into the hallway, daggers flying in all directions. "Janice, next time I expect you not to allow any disruptions."

"Hey, Mr. Holden." Noel's chipper voice greeted us as he approached. He extended his hand out to my boss. "It's so good to see you again."

"You too." But the sour expression said otherwise.

Noel rocked on his heels. "We missed Bentley last night."

Daniel flipped his gaze between Noel and I, but he ended back on Noel, narrowing his eyes like a lion seeking his prey. "We?"

"Yes, the school, and his class. He was my best tenor."

"Oh, yes, that. Well, his mother wasn't feeling great, so he stayed home." Daniel huffed and pushed out his chest. "Miss Edwards, I'll need you in my office shortly to finish this up." He waved the folder. No doubt he was turning as blue as the paper.

"Of course." I turned my attention to Noel, after seeing the smirk fall off Janice's face. She wasn't stupid. She knew exactly what went on behind locked doors, of that I was 100% sure. "Mr. Sullivan, please come in." I escorted him into my grand office and closed the door, leaving it unlocked.

"Wow, this almost as big as my classroom and it's just for you. You even have a huge Christmas tree."

I laughed as I glanced around. My office wasn't as nearly as big as Daniel's, but it was large enough to contain a long desk, two comfy chairs in front of it and a small couch along the windowed wall where the tree sat in all its decorated glory. The view of the downtown core was exquisite, especially in the early hours when the sun rose.

"It's almost too big. Almost." I stopped in front of the small hutch where I had a microwave and a small fridge. Working through lunch was more common than I'd like. "Can I get you anything?"

"No. No, thank you." He was like a child in a candy store, wide eyed with wonder as he took it all in, thrusting his hands into the pockets of his black jeans.

"So, Noel, what brings you out this way?" I walked around to my side of the desk and sat, kicking the wastebasket further under my desk.

"Well… You."

"Me?"

"I didn't like the way things ended last night, and when I went home, I'll admit I did some Googling on you."

That was a first. As so far as I knew, no one aside from employers, and me on occasion, had bothered to search for me on the internet. "And?"

"I liked what I saw and read."

"Which would be?" I raised an eyebrow and crossed my legs. There were a few things for him to choose from, but I was curious what had caught his eye most.

"Your philanthropy."

Which was minimal in the grand scheme of things. Years ago, I'd been drawn to a foundation designed to help counsel women and their children who had been exposed to domestic violence, thanks to a friend who had the unfortunate need for it. Once I learned about it, it was something I knew in my heart I needed to donate to.

"As sweet as that is, I'm not buying it. You didn't come all the way down here because of the donations to any foundation."

"You're right." He straightened his thick jean jacket as he slipped into a chair before me and cleared his throat. "It's more than that. I'm interested, and for reasons I can't get out of my head, I think you're interested as well."

My voice cracked at his statement. "Why? Why would you think that?" I swallowed and quickly flicked the ripped condom wrapper I'd absently left near my keyboard onto the floor, praying Noel hadn't caught sight of it.

"You got me thinking, see. Last week, I suspected something, a curiosity if you will. But when you showed up last night to the concert without a child, well, something inside of me just sort of started connecting the dots. I figured, maybe she is interested. So, I asked you out and you said yes."

"In my defence, you did invite me."

"Fair enough, but I thought you'd be joining the Holden Family."

"We don't socialize together outside of work." I gathered the papers sitting on my desk and filed in the tomorrow bin. So much for getting them to the courts today. It would have to be first on my to-do list in the morning, otherwise, there'd be hell to pay.

"I know."

"How?"

"Because last week was the first time I'd ever met you. I'd never forget someone as lovely as you." Just the sweet way he spoke melted me like butter.

My lips curled into a grin. "You're smooth." I winked. "So why did you come all this way to see me again?"

He hadn't answered the question, but he got an A+ in deflection.

"I was wondering if you had plans tonight?"

I was due to Daniel's office two minutes ago, plus I had a couple small projects I needed to accomplish, but other than that... "No. Nothing important."

"Could I interest you in a little shopping and perhaps an appetizer?" He rose and breached my personal zone, standing a little too close, but yet, I wasn't uncomfortable.

"Appetizer?" Was that code for something?

"Remember last night when I said I did coffee first, and not the dinner? This is the step in between. Perhaps we could grab a tea and a scone and window shop?"

His thumb stroked my knuckles and took my breath away. "Umm, sure. Shopping and scones would be absolutely lovely." I broke the gaze and refocused on my computer screen. "Give me a few minutes to finish this?"

"Whatever you need."

My hand turned cold the second he let go. "Help yourself to anything."

"I'll just check out this to die for view." He meandered over to the huge windows and whistled as he stared out, absently calling out the names of the well-known buildings.

In record time, I saved my files, tidied my desk, and stared at the clothes hanging on the back of my door, thankful to have remembered to brought jeans and a nice sweater with me this morning. "Alright, done for today. Let me just change."

"I'll give you some privacy."

I hardly had time to tell him I'd just use the executive washroom when he was already out in the hall, closing the door behind him. Through the frosted glass, his voice rang out as he chatted with Janice. My heart thrumming loudly in my chest, I quickly changed out of my pencil skirt, pantyhose and heels, and pulled on a pair of skinny jeans and my knee-high boots. I replaced my blouse with a gorgeous emerald cable knit sweater. Somehow, I pulled off the transition as I gazed into the mirror on the back of the door.

I looked ready to hit the mall and not a board meeting.

Shit. Daniel. What was I going to do about that? I had really wanted to finish the job, and have the favour returned, but now? And I wanted an answer to my question – would I get it? My shoulders slumped knowing he would likely divert. He was a master manipulator – I'd seen that side of him in business meetings all the time.

I paused and stared at the lady in the mirror. Had I been manipulated? Had he been using me? No, it wasn't possible, I would've noticed. I was smarter than that. And yet… I couldn't help but make comparisons between Noel and Daniel.

A different offer had been presented in the form of Noel and I'd be a fool to put this on hold, to see what his deal was.

In the morning, I'd make it up to Daniel. I'd wear my sexiest black underwear and my see-through demi-cup bra. That would rebuild his fire.

Mine too. Especially if he said yes.

With my jacket on and my purse tucked under my arm, I inhaled to calm my racing heart and blinked twice to settle my nerves. For the first time in a long while, I was pumped to leave the office early, and with someone who wasn't my boss.

Six

*T*urns out Noel was quite the shopper. I followed him in and out of a dozen different stores, and he took my suggestions on what to get some of his colleagues, putting down the scented candles and fancy coffee mugs everyone was likely to get from their students. Noel bought a gift for every one of his twenty-eight students and forty-three staff members.

The only people at the office I bought gifts for were Janice, my unfailing secretary, a couple of other employees under my direct authority, and Daniel, who had a special naughty gift coming his way. Otherwise, Holden Enterprises took care of dispensing the gifts, usually in the form of bonuses and gift cards, nothing personal like Noel was buying.

His generosity was unmatched.

The shopping completed, he left me standing by a water fountain as he quickly ran his purchases out to his vehicle. Breathlessly, he made his way over to me a few minutes later. "Sorry for keeping you waiting." From behind his back, he pulled out a pink rose and handed it to me. "For you. Thank you for helping me."

My heart swelled. How sweet was he? "Thanks was more than enough. It's nice to be away from the office. I've never had the honour of helping anyone shop before." I lifted the single flower to my nose and breathed in its sweet scent. "Where did you get this?"

"There's a flower shop at the entrance."

It wasn't even planned; he had made an impulsive purchase. "It's lovely. Thank you."

Noel looked down at his runners and kicked a smidgen of snow from his shoes. "Can I interest you in a scone?"

"Aren't you hungrier than that?"

He shrugged, but a smile built beneath the

whiskers, giving him a five o'clock shadow.

"Are we okay to grab dinner?" It was bold of me to presume, but after the fun shopping and now the rose, I'd hoped we'd moved to his dinner level kind of get together.

"I'd like that." The grin deepened, tugging on the bottom of his eyes.

"Brewhouse?" I pointed to the first place I spotted – a national chain restaurant.

"Too loud. Plus, it's a sports bar so you can't really hear the other person talk."

"Fair enough. Where to?"

"Do you like eating with your fingers?"

I narrowed my eyes in a half smile. "What did you have in mind?"

Had it come from Daniel, it would've been a double-entendre, but coming from the sweet Noel, it was likely an innocent question.

"There's a great seafood place on the north wing."

Without hesitation, I nodded. "Let's do it."

We walked side by side, getting into the busier section of the mall. The Christmas music playing overhead wasn't as audible, but the hum from the pushier crowd was. I was getting bumped left and right, until Noel swapped places with me, putting me next to the shop windows as he took the knocks. It was a friendly gesture, and his free hand found its way to mine, tangling our fingers together.

As if suddenly drenched in ice water, I froze in place and my eyes widened.

"Sorry, too fast?"

For a heartbeat, it had felt natural. Then I remembered who I was with, and where I was. "You just caught me off guard."

"Did I now?"

This whole everything with Noel was throwing me for a loop. Being in his presence brought a calm to my spirit I hadn't felt before, and as much as it felt right, it felt wrong too.

"Yeah."

He bridged the already narrow gap between us. "I'm sorry. For coming on too strong. It…you… I just feel…" His gaze dropped. "I forgot you had someone."

Until he touched my hand, that *someone* hadn't surfaced in my head. I hadn't even looked at my phone either.

"Like I said, it's complicated. Probably

more than it should be."

He was so close I noticed the different coloured flecks of brown in his irises, and my pulse zoomed in response to sharing the same air as him. A part of me begged to brush against his lips, while another laughed at the very idea because it was deeply personal, and I was pretty damn sure we were not even remotely close to being there.

"You really are unexpected, Britannia."

"I'll take that as a compliment."

"You absolutely should."

Playfully, he nudged my arm, and cocked his head to the interior of the mall. With the odd sideways gaze, we made it to the restaurant, where we were sat in the back, away from the noise and buzz of the mall.

"If you'll excuse me." He hopped out of his seat after placing his drink order, his ringing phone firmly in his grip.

Which reminded me… I pulled my own out and stared at numerous text messages. Seventy-four to be exact. Three from a friend I hadn't spoken to since Thanksgiving, so I paid it no further attention, two were from my mother reminding me of the family Christmas party on

Saturday, and the rest were from Daniel.

As I quickly scrolled, there were only two pictures, and one was captioned *had to take care of business myself.* I laughed, amazed by the idea he had time to photograph the end of the job. I closed out of the picture and skimmed over the remaining messages, most inquiring where I'd gone and how he missed me. But he never answered my question.

The last text came in a few minutes ago. *Come see me tomorrow morning.*

I wasn't sure of the tone. Was it sent in anger? Or did he just miss me so much, that we needed to redo what we started in my office? I was perplexed but pushed the thought away for now.

"Everything okay?" Noel slid into the seat across from me.

With a quick flick, I closed out of the messages. "I should ask you that?"

He nodded. "Sorry, that was my sister. When Holly calls, I need to drop what I'm doing."

"Wait a second, you have a sister named Holly?"

"Yeah, do you know her?" His head tipped to the side.

No. There was nothing familiar about a

Holly Sullivan, however, I chuckled all the same. "Was she born around Christmas?"

Now he got where I was going with my questioning, and he shifted in his seat as a broad grin stretched out from ear to ear. "Yes. Four days before. Her birthday is on Friday."

"And yours is?"

Slowly, he tipped his head down. "It was yesterday."

"Oh, my goodness." My eyes went as wide as saucers, and I flagged down our server. "Yesterday was this man's birthday. Can you add two crème Brulés to our order? We're going to celebrate. And change my diet coke into a glass of chardonnay, please."

Without a word, our server disappeared.

Noel was bright flame red all across his cheeks, and it spread into his hair line. "We really don't have to celebrate my birthday. Besides it's already over."

"Nonsense, you can celebrate your birthday for a full week if you do it right."

"When's yours, so I can do that very thing?"

"I guess you'll find out in time." I winked

as the server set down a tall glass of red. I lifted it to Noel's beer. "Cheers. To the happiest of birthdays."

"To the magic of the season."

Buttery crab legs and scrumptious shrimp filled my tummy, and my head was full from an evening of laughter and fantastic conversation. It had been far too long since I'd enjoyed both a savoury meal and witty words with a male counterpart. After the initial hand holding attempt, and my declaration of all things complicated, that fell to the wayside. Being with Noel was as easy as breathing. For the first time in forever, I wasn't mentally preparing some script to be played while out from behind closed doors, I was allowed to roam, be wild, and breathe. I loved every minute of it.

After the meal, Noel insisted on safely delivering me to my car, despite my assurance I'd be just fine. We walked the length of the mall until we arrived at the double glass entrance doors, where just beyond, the snow was falling in big fat flakes.

"Wow, would you look at that?"

"That's really something." Noel pulled on a knitted toque and slipped his hand into a pair of leather gloves.

I too, bundled up, but rather than put on a hat that would flatten my hair, I pulled my hood overtop, hoping I looked as cute as the model had on the website I'd ordered the jacket from. I grabbed my phone, and flipped away a few more messages from Daniel, and opened the app for my car, telling it to start warming up.

"You sure do get a lot of messages."

I slipped the phone back into my purse and shifted the pink rose into my other hand. "My boss."

"He must be quite the micromanager to be constantly pinging you. My principal trusts me enough to not message me once the workday is done. There has to be some down time."

Suddenly, my feathers were ruffled, and I went on the defensive. "It's not that, as he's great with the work and lets me do my own thing."

"So, it's personal then?"

There was a skeptical look on his face I didn't like, and I tugged my sleeves down and pulled my hands in as far as I could while still holding the rose and my purse. When Daniel messaged me after work had finished for the day, it was hardly business related. It was about us, the crap his wife was putting him through, how tired he was of her behaviour, but how he just needed to find the right way to tell her it was over.

"Sorry, I overstepped."

I turned my head away as I wasn't going to go there since it was none of Noel's business what happened between Daniel and me. My view left his handsome face and watched the snowflakes as they danced to the ground.

"Well, thank you for a lovely evening." My hand was braced on the door, and my stomach was clenching tightly to my heart. "My car's just out there, so I'll be fine from here."

"And there I go sticking my nose into someone else's business, ruining the fun time we'd had." His chin tucked into his chest. "Come on, I'll walk you out to your car."

"I'm good, honestly."

Did I wish him a Merry Christmas like I would a retail employee I had no intention of seeing again? How did I end this and say goodbye? Because I really didn't want it to end, I enjoyed my time with him, and it felt great to be me and not the workaholic me, or the lady at Daniel's beck and call.

"Have a good night." It was the only sensible thing to come to mind as I pushed open the door and inhaled a blast of frosty air.

"I said I'd make sure you got into your car safely. I'm a man of my word." He shivered as he stepped out into the crisp December air.

The snow absorbed all the sound and the mall usually alive with a hum and buzz had fallen silent under the wintery skies. It was breathtaking and mesmerizing.

A few steps later, and we were beside my car where I deactivated the alarm. "This is me."

Noel stopped just short of my car and cleared a path with his foot in the freshly fallen snow. "Until I put my foot in my mouth, I had a good time tonight."

"Me too."

"And I'm sorry if my nosiness put a damper on things."

"It's fine." But it wasn't. I was in love with Daniel, and he was in my every thought.

Except...

Tonight, he really wasn't. At least not much or only when I checked my phone. What did that mean?

The snow continued to fall, flakes dancing all around us. I watched, captivated, as a sizeable one floated around and caught on the edge of Noel's incredibly long lashes. As he tried to blink it away, it moved up and down.

My warm finger reached up to melt it, and I stared deep into his expressive dark brown eyes. Once again, I warred with brushing my lips over his, but knew it was too personal for two people to kiss when they hardly knew each other. I'd been banging my boss for months and had yet been given the chance to taste his lips. But this wasn't Daniel. Countless moments over the three times I've been with him, he'd shown me how different he was.

Could I do it? Could I be bold enough to make the first move?

My gaze danced all over his face, moving from his soulful eyes, down over his whiskery cheeks and settling on his perfectly pink lips. In a daring move, I stood on my tip toes and pressed my trembling lips onto his.

Noel did not disappoint. He returned my kiss, taunting and testing to see how far I'd go, and in the middle of the parking lot in the height of a snowfall, I took it to a personal level. My arms wrapped around his neck, the rose petals rubbed against his ear, and he braced his hands on the window behind me, gently kissing my lips until they swelled as much as my heart.

I was in deep trouble. Yep, deep, deep trouble.

Seven

I'd barely slept a wink last night, as my mind replayed the evening over and over again, like a highlight reel. I tried to hide the dark circles and bags under mounds of concealer, but it was useless. A train wreck looked better.

When Janice popped her head into my office as she arrived, she did a double take. "Everything okay?"

"Oh sure." I padded the packed luggage under my eyes. "Just had a lot on my mind." Mostly Noel, which surprised me. That kiss really did a number on my heart and mind.

"I've got something for that." She

disappeared, only to return a few minutes later. "I picked it up yesterday and forgot to take it out of my bag." She handed me an expensive looking jar with rose-gold coloured font circling the beige jar. "It's not a brand name, but it really works. Try one under each eye."

I set the jar down, nodding. "Thank you." I lifted an envelope. "I'm nearly finished with this, and it needs to be couriered over to the courthouse."

"I'll make the arrangements right now." She paused at the entrance to the office. "Have you seen Mr. Holden yet?"

I'd been putting that off, however I knew he always arrived around seven-thirty-three – nearly a half hour ago – and I hadn't heard hide or hair from him. A storm was brewing.

"No, not yet. Why?"

"He's on a war path this morning. Fired Jennings."

"Over what?" I zipped through the possible reasonings to let someone go and drew a blank when it came to Jennings. She had been an all-star receptionist.

Janice shrugged. "Just be… careful."

"I always am."

"I like the rose, by the way."

I'd brought the pink rose in this morning. For some reason, it looked perfect on the corner of my desk, and I loved the warm feeling it stirred in my gut when I looked upon it. "Thanks. It was a gift."

"But not from Mr. Holden." Her eyes went large, and she slapped a hand over her mouth.

I jumped out of my chair and ushered her in, closing the door behind her. "I guess that's not much of a secret, is it?"

Eyes still wide, she shook her head.

"Damn." I paced back and forth from my desk to the view of downtown. "How much do you know?"

"About you two?"

It was said in such a way, I tipped my head to the side, curious about her tone. An unsettled feeling washed over me. I swallowed down my fear and stared her dead in the eye. "Are there others?"

"I can't say."

"Can't or won't?"

"Both. I need this job, please don't fire me, Miss Edwards." There was such a plea in her voice, it caught me off guard. That and it came from way out of left field.

Since I'd been an employee of Holden Enterprises, I'd only fired two people, and both were deserved.

"I have zero intentions of firing you. Your job performance has been exemplary." I crossed my arms over my chest.

Her shoulders sagged with relief. "Thank you."

"When did you know?"

A sadness covered her face. "We've always known."

We've – which meant more than just her. Fantastic. "Thank you, Janice. I'll be DND for the rest of the day."

Suddenly, I didn't want to talk to or see anyone. How embarrassing to find out everyone knew of my situation with Daniel? I thought we'd been private about that. Locked doors and all.

A knock sounded on my door a couple of hours later, and I rose to go and answer. Do Not Disturb meant exactly that, and as I yanked open the door ready to tear someone a new one, I was assaulted by the scent of a dozen red roses sitting in Janice's arms.

"Sorry for the intrusion," her voice was soft and apologetic, "but these just came for you special delivery and as much as I would enjoy smelling them all day, they really belong in here with you."

"Thank you." I took the gorgeous bouquet from her hands. "Who are they from?"

"The driver didn't say, just that they were for you."

My focus couldn't leave the velvety flowers and the aroma was intoxicating. What a truly sweet surprise, and although I suspected who they were from, I wasn't 100% sure. Last night Noel gave me a single pink rose, could these have come from him as well? I set the flowers on the table and hunted for the card. Tearing open the envelope, my heart burst at the seams seeing Noel's name scribbled on the bottom.

"Are they from that nice guy who was here yesterday?" Her whole face brightened with her question.

"Yes," I barely breathed out.

"And that's from him too?" She was pointing at the long-stemmed pink rose.

I nodded.

"He's dreamy, that one." Blushing, she smiled. Without another word, she closed the door as she exited.

I rushed over to my desk and dialled the number on the bottom of the card from my cell phone, and not from the office line.

With luck, he answered on the second ring.

"Thank you for the embarrassing display of red roses."

"I'm so glad you got them. Never know if the company actually delivers them or if they just take the money and run."

"Had an issue with these places before?" I cocked an eyebrow, not that he could see, and gently ran my finger over the soft petals.

"Nah. I've never used them, but my VP recommended this one."

"Well, they arrived, and they are stunning. You really shouldn't have." A couple had bloomed, stretching out their petals in full glory.

"It was my pleasure. Thank you for last night. I meant it when I said I had a good time."

Remembering the kiss, under the falling snow, sent a wave of heat over my chest. "Me too."

"I have a work gathering Friday night.

Would you be interested in joining me?" There was a hitch in his voice and a long pause as I contemplated my choices.

Meeting his colleagues was a huge step. "Like a date-date?"

His laughter filled the other end of the line. "Yeah, like a date. But if it makes it easier, you could use your fallback term of a get together."

A soft chuckle rolled out of me until a movement from the corner of my eye caught my attention. My door was opening, and it wasn't Janice. It was Daniel.

"Can I call you back?" The fun in my voice dropped faster than a hot potato.

"Everything okay?"

"Perfect. I'll call you back in twenty minutes." I ended the call before Noel could ask anymore questions.

Daniel stepped into my office, hand firmly on the doorknob, his gaze laser focused on the bouquet of roses. "Who are those from?"

I refused to answer, and I didn't have to.

"They're from Bentley's teacher, aren't they?" The expression on his face turned cold as ice as he bellowed from the doorway. "Janice, we'll be in a meeting. Unless the building is on fire, do not disturb." He shut the door with a little force, securing the locking mechanism. "You never did come by my office yesterday."

"I had a few things of urgency to finish."

"I should've been on that list. I hate being cockblocked." There was a tsk on the tip of his tongue. "And you're usually so good at relieving the pressure. Instead, I had to do the job myself and it's no fun with just your picture to look at."

Right, the picture. Or pictures as it would be. He had taken a few fairly flattering ones when I had worn my sexiest bra and panties. At least I was semi-naked, unlike the photos he'd sent me.

I rocked back in my chair and stared up at him, unsure of what to do or say next. Any other day, I likely would've given in and fixed the situation. Even as I'd left last night, I'd thought about wearing a sexy pair thong and garter belt just for him this morning, but somewhere along the way, something changed. Today I'd selected items for me, and not anyone else, and by god, it was great to be comfortable.

"Last night I called and called, but you wouldn't answer." He stalked over to my desk and sat on the corner of it, pushing the papers I had sorted neatly into a mess in the centre of my workspace.

"I was out."

Dark eyes settled over my face. "I needed you, like I need you now." He reached for my hand and brought it to his lips, licking and sucking on my fingertips. Despite my desire to not engage with him at the moment, my body betrayed me, and a dull ache nestled in between my thighs, growing deeper the longer my finger stayed in his mouth. "Only you make me happy." He pressed his firming erection into the palm of my hand. "Let's finish what we started yesterday. Please."

The ache intensified as he pulled me to my feet and brought me close, wrapping me in his expensive cologne. However, for the first time in six months, it repulsed me.

"You know you need me too." His hand ran along my back and over my ass, squeezing it tightly before he started hiking up the bottom of my skirt.

"Stop." The firmest voice I'd ever given life to roared out. A flat palm braced against his chest. "I said stop."

Like a bolt of lightning struck him, his hand

fell away. "Oh, are you on the rag?"

I blew a gust of air out. "Get out. Get out of my office."

I smoothed the back of my skirt and stepped around to the other side of my desk, out in the open where I wasn't trapped in a corner.

"Where is this coming from, Brit?" His voice was smooth and low.

But I'd had enough. All night long, I thought about how much of a gentleman Noel was, how he walked on the outside of mall traffic to take the bumps, the rose, and how he made me laugh and forget about work. And that snowflake kiss... It was personal. He made it personal, and I adored that about him.

"Answer me honestly, Daniel... Do you love me?" It was rare to use his name, and his head pushed back upon hearing it.

"Brit, you know I do."

"Say it. Say the words." Hearing them would change everything, but the nagging sensation in my gut told me they were never going to be vocalised.

"What words are you wanting me to say?"

"Tell me you love me."

"I already have." He slipped off the corner of the desk and rose to his full height.

I shook my head as an anger I should've seen coming fueled into life. "No, you haven't."

He readjusted himself, the once rising part of him losing its stronghold but he took no action to touch me this time. "What's this all about? You know how I feel about you."

"Fine, you claim you love me, so let's go out onto the floor holding hands. Let's go tell the staff about us then." I marched past him over to the door, ready to yank it open.

"Don't you dare!"

The tone sent a chill down my back and my hand froze on the handle.

"Because you don't love me, right? You're never going to leave her. You're never going to pick me and love me, right?" Like a knife to the heart, my own words gutted me.

They had to be truth as Daniel wasn't moving, and his face had zero trace of sympathy. It was obvious now, he'd been using me in some sort of sick fantasy and feeding me full of lies, and the gullible idiot I was, I believed every word, falling hook, line, and sinker.

"I'm married, what do you expect? That I'm just going to leave my wife of fifteen years." His gaze roamed up and down my body. "For you?"

Yes, that was exactly what I expected.

"You're a whore, willing to sleep your way to the top."

My pulse screamed as it jumped a notch and the adrenaline coursing through my veins powered me over to him. "That's a god damn lie, and you know it. I worked my ass off to get to the top, and any of my former employers would back that up."

"Yeah, well…" He stormed around the room. "I have dirty pictures of you." He reduced himself to a petulant child, ready to stick out his tongue as if that would give extra weight to his words. It surprised me how long it took to see what a bad, dirty man he truly was.

I laughed in Daniel's face. Sure, I'd be embarrassed if they ever got out, but not horribly. I wasn't naked in any because I'd refused to let it go that far, and the pictures were more tasteful than a spread in Playboy, that was for sure; more like an ad for Victoria's secret.

"Mine are so much cleaner than yours, borderline classy. You know how many dick pics I have on my phone? All coming from you. All geo-tagged to your location. Wouldn't your wife like to see?"

The colour dropped out of his face. "You wouldn't?"

Truth was, no I wouldn't stoop to that level. Not unless I was severely pushed, but he didn't know that.

"Try me." I folded my arms across my chest.

A new colour filled his face; maroon flushed from the opening in his shirt collar straight over his nose and cheeks and into his hairline. "You're fired."

"On what grounds?"

"On being a total bitch."

Yeah, that wasn't going to sit well with HR. We both knew it, and I laughed at the idea of him calling down and saying as much. Instead, I walked over to the phone, lifted the handset, and held my finger over the buttons. "Do you want to let HR know I'm fired, and on what grounds?"

Defeated, he stormed over to the door and

blew through it like a tornado, taking anyone out in his path.

Once I was sure he was out of earshot, I slumped down onto my sofa and leaned my head back on it in relief. After a few calming breaths, I took a quick inventory around my office. A few boxes worth of personal effects could be easily packed up, if that was the road I was willing to take. Rather than debate it, I headed over to my desk and picked up my cell phone.

"Good timing," Noel's welcoming voice greeted me. "I'm just getting ready to head back to class."

"Lucky for me."

"Are you okay? You sound funny."

I glanced around the space again. "Before I say yes to the date-date and meet your co-workers, can we get together for a coffee beforehand? There are a couple of things I'd like to discuss with you first."

His swallow was audible. "Sure. How about that indie café?"

"Perfect." We squared away the details and hung up.

Just one more call to make. Hands shaking,

Noel

I lifted the phone out of the cradle and dialled
Janice.

    "Yes, Miss Edwards?"

"Can you put me through to Human Resources?"

Eight

Sitting in the tiny coffee shop, I flipped my phone over in my hands and bounced my leg under the table. I was more nervous in this moment than I had been for several takeovers. The butterflies swarmed at top speed and the pounding was so rampant in my ears, I barely heard the Christmas music playing overhead.

The bells above the door jungled, grabbing my attention for the briefest of moments, until my eyes settled over the handsome Mr. Sullivan as he waltzed in looking as marvelous as ever.

He stood before me. "Hi."

"Hi," I breathed out as a smile leaked out

the sides of my lips.

He leaned forward and hesitated, and I beat him to the punch, hopefully removing his doubt, by placing my lip-gloss-coated lips over his. Pulling away and staring deep into my eyes, he sighed. "A guy could get used to a greeting like that." The twinkle in his dark eyes made my heart skip a beat. "I'm going to love showing you off on Friday night." He cocked his head. "It's going to be in our gym at seven, so I really should pick you up."

"About that." I waved for him to sit, a habit of many boardroom visits. But as I gazed into his soul, he wasn't an acquisition. He was real. So very real. A fantasy come true. I swallowed and pushed a steamy mug of hot chocolate toward him.

"Why am I suddenly nervous?"

"You have no reason to be, this is all on me. In the interest of full disclosure, there are a few things I need to clear the air about." I inhaled a sharp scent of cinnamon as I lifted my mug and stole a quick sip.

"Okay."

What I was about to reveal was incredibly difficult, but I enjoyed this man's company and he deserved to know what kind of person I truly was.

I sighed; the kind that sounds worst than it should be.

Noel reached across the tiny table and wrapped his hands around mine. "Whatever it is, it can't be that big."

"It is." I searched his face for any warning sign of not proceeding, but he was leaning close and taking me all in. "The thing is, Noel, is I'm a home-wrecker."

He pulled back but still continued to hold my hand. "What do you mean?"

"The phone calls from my boss... well..." God, it was so hard to admit, which was silly, because hadn't I wanted to announce to the world how I was banging my boss and how he'd left his beautiful wife for me? "They were... of a personal nature."

His face fell.

In one swoop, the layers I was hiding behind were peeled away exposing me raw.

"For the past six months, I've been with..." But I couldn't say his name, and I hung my head in shame.

"You've been screwing Daniel Holden? Bentley's father?" The roaring disgust echoed through the empty coffee shop.

"Yes."

"Wow." In a quick move, he retracted his hands and rocked back on two legs of his chair.

I set my cooling, yet sweaty palms into my lap and stared at the hot chocolate. "As much as I want to blame Daniel for it, it was all on me. It doesn't matter if I believed his lies when he said he was leaving her for me, I still willingly had relations with a married man." Hearing those words killed a part of me.

"A very happily married man."

With that, I snapped my gaze in his direction, and the unbroken parts of my heart burst apart.

"Mr. and Mrs. Holden are huge donors to the school. They maybe don't attend every school event, but they are at every meet the teacher night and parent-teacher interviews, and if there's a charity event you can bet your last dollar, Mrs. Holden is there. I never thought for one moment they were a struggling couple and were separating." He broke eye contact and let it fall away. "How could you get involved with him like that?"

I shrugged, not fully understanding how it progressed to that. One day we were boss and assistant, and in the blink of an eye, we'd had sex on the boardroom table. "I honestly don't know. At first, I didn't even know they were married. I'd only been with Holden Enterprises for a year, and I wasn't even working under Daniel, until about eight months ago. He wore no wedding ring, and until he mentioned Bentley's fourth grade teacher last June, I honestly didn't know he was married. But we'd already been together."

"And you didn't think to end it when you found out?"

"I didn't know what to do." Using my pointer fingernail, I pushed back the cuticles on my opposite hand until they were red and raw. "As time went on, he mentioned he was leaving her, and he wanted to be with me. He promised."

"And that spurred you on, didn't it? He whispered all the right words and you gobbled it up. Believed he was going to give up a marriage for you."

Until I saw the sneer pinching his left cheek, I thought he was on my side and seeing it the way I had.

"You know what happens to guys who cheat on their wives? They'll cheat on their next wife too. Things wouldn't have been any different."

"I know that now." The old saying, once a cheater, always a cheater ran through loud and clear. I hoped the saying wasn't true for homewreckers.

"What was your reasoning in telling me this?" He took a long drink from his hot chocolate and slammed the cup down on the saucer, dribbles of dark milk running down the sides.

"Because today there was an incident at work. Between Daniel and I. Human Resources is involved."

Noel snapped his head up. "Did he?"

"He didn't do anything and when I said stop, he respected that."

His shoulders fell and rolled inward.

"But I contacted HR to see what my options were, as Daniel threatened to fire me although there was no good reason, and then threatened to leak scantily clad photos of me." I hadn't revealed all of that to the guy in human resources though, that would've been career suicide.

Plus, Daniel hadn't said he'd *actually* leak the pics in those words, but the intention was clear enough. If he ever did, my revenge would be greater, although I'd be hard pressed to actually do it. I didn't hate the man. I had been in love with him. Once.

"Okay."

I brushed away Noel's one-word response and took a chance on staring up into those soulful eyes, only now they held as much disgust for me as I held for myself. "I just wanted you to know. You'd mentioned early on how you couldn't spend time with someone if it wasn't reciprocated, and how you'd written the book on rejection."

"What are you saying?"

I inhaled to a count of three and exhaled just as slowly. "I'm saying I'm through with Daniel and I'm ready to move on." My eyes searched his. "With you." My breath froze in my chest as I waited for his response.

His face tightened and he propped his ankle onto his knee while staring in my direction. The more the pained beats between us added up, the tighter the gut clenching became.

"You want to move on with me?"

I nodded like a bobble head toy.

"While I appreciate your honesty, and frankly, it was a little disturbing, I think I'm going to pass on *moving on*." He pushed his mug toward the centre of the table. "I don't want to be the guy someone settles for, and I don't want to be in second place by default."

Which couldn't have been further from the truth.

"I though you were different, and I honestly believed you had appeared in my life due to some magical Christmas spirit destiny bullshit." Standing abruptly, he tightened his jacket. "It was nice meeting you, Britannia. I hope you find the one person who fills your heart with happiness and who gets excited at the mere thought of seeing you. Someone like…" He paused and stomped his foot. "Anyway, have a Merry Christmas."

My view blurred, but it was clear enough to watch in silence as Noel exited the coffee shop and out of sight. Instantly, an ache formed in my chest and the notion I'd disappointed Noel hurt more than Daniel's name calling a few hours ago.

Nine

My closet beckoned me and perusing a variety of festive wear, I settled on the ugly sweater I'd purchased two days ago. It was the ugliest thing I could find, given the exceptionally limited selection but it would do its intended job. Also, my desperate hunt for one particular item, led me into a dollar store, where I found the topping on the cake accessory needed for tonight.

Dressed in skinny jeans, knee high boots and my god-awful sweater, I arrived at the prep school, this time with more luck in the parking situation, since it was after seven and this was a staff-only event. I cringed internally hoping I wasn't making the world's second biggest mistake in showing up unannounced, my first being that I had hooked up with the likes of Daniel Holden.

I buzzed at the main entrance and waited. Peering into the windows, the hall was deserted. Why shouldn't it be? The staff weren't hanging around there. For good measure, I buzzed again.

What luck! A lady about my age, in an attractive, black, full-length dress, walked over to the door. "Can I help you?"

"Yes, you can. I'm here for the party."

Rightfully so, she raised an eyebrow.

"I mean, I'm here for Noel. With Noel. I'm just running late." My thoughts were all smashed together.

"Noel hasn't yet arrived."

I took a step back. "Oh. He is coming though, right?" My plan hinged on him being at the school and if he wasn't, well, I was up shit creek without a paddle.

"I'm afraid I can't answer that."

Of course, she couldn't, FOIP laws and all that, which I understood. For all she knew, I was a crazy psycho, which was likely not far off based on Noel's last assessment.

"That's fine. I'll text him and find out." I waved my phone in the air, acting like Noel and I had planned on me showing up. "Thanks." Not wanting to leave the warmth of the area, I stood for just a breath longer and backed up. "I'll grab a hot chocolate and wait."

"You do that." She let the door close and latch but didn't go anywhere.

Slowly, I turned around and made my way down the sidewalk toward my car. I scanned the area, shivering from the dampness in the air, and if I was being honest, a little from the rejection as I had been expecting Noel to be here. Sighing, I slipped into the warm interior of my car and waited a few more minutes. Not seeing him at all, I put the car into gear and starting driving.

At first it was aimless, and the GPS was directing me back home, making course corrections as I turned left, when I should've turned right. But I didn't want to go home. Not yet. Instead, I pulled in front of *Chai One On* and walked inside.

The place was dead but given how it was a Friday night and there was a snowfall warning for tomorrow, maybe most decided to stay home.

However, the scent of fresh ground coffee and a mixture of spices hung in the air, giving me a comfort I wasn't expecting. I walked up to the counter and placed my order to the cute little barista who'd made eyes at Noel, ordering Noel's hot chocolate which had become a new favourite.

"Can I just use your bathroom?"

The barista pointed to a corridor in the back of the tiny café.

While my hot chocolate was brewing, I went to the ladies' room. It had been a rough couple of days, and I'd really hoped seeing Noel would take the edge off. After my conversation with HR, and the disaster of my last get together with Noel, I'd done a lot of thinking. I took a sick day and spent all of it working out the situation. And all this morning. After a morning of avoidance, I walked into my office, packed up my personal effects and put them into my car. Telling Daniel I was leaving was the hardest part, and professionally, face to face was the only way to go, but with doors wide open. I didn't care who knew I was leaving. Turns out the only one who was upset was Janice.

Since I was taking the time off between

Christmas and New Years, there was no point to coming in on Monday, especially since our private meeting was now off the table so my Christmas vacation started a few hours early.

Shoulders back with my cheeks freshly pinched to bring some much-needed colour to them, I exited the restroom and walked back into the café, my feet sticking in place at the sight of Noel leaning against the counter.

Assessing him, I wasn't sure if I should walk over, if I should say hi from a distance, or just grab my hot chocolate and get the hell out of there without a word. I was usually so confident around men, but there was something about Noel that turned me into a teenage girl with a giddy crush.

He looked up from the counter and slowly turned to me, nodding.

"Hey." The tone was flat, making him even harder to read.

My feet remained glued to the spot. "Hey."

A baristo pushed the takeaway drink my way. "Your hot chocolate's ready."

"Thanks." But I made no effort to grab it, my full attention was on the handsome man walking toward me.

"You like the hot chocolate, eh?"

I nodded, my mouth growing drier by the heartbeat.

"My co-worker mentioned some lady showed up ringing the front door of the school looking for me, was that you?"

I scanned his face. The twinkle in his eyes was there, as was a small smirk forming on the edge of his perfectly kissable lips. Swallowing, I starred into his dark browns. "Guilty as charged."

"You didn't stick around."

"I did, for a bit, but you never showed."

"By the time Maria told me I'd had a visitor, you were already gone."

My jaw dropped. "You were there? Why didn't she go and tell you? Why lie about it?"

"You haven't figured that out?"

I shook my head, not understanding at all.

"Maria has the hots for me and was hoping to change the field from professional to personal, however, I don't mix business and pleasure."

Was that a shot to me? The blank expression on his face gave nothing away. "How did you know I was here?"

"She mentioned something about a hot

chocolate, and when I pulled into the parking lot, I saw your car. Teslas aren't popular out here."

At least that part of the equation was solved, but before I could ask, Noel started.

"Why did you show up at the school though? I thought it was clear nothing further would happen between us."

I nodded and tucked a strand of hair behind my ears. "Some things are worth fighting for?"

"Oh yeah?"

"Yeah." I chanced a small grin. "Why'd you come looking for me?"

Noel directed me over to a tiny table and pulled out a chair for me.

"Thank you." I sat and crossed my legs. "You were about to answer?"

"I've had time to think it through. As corny as it sounds, the thought of not seeing you again rattled me. I debated stopping by your office, but obviously, never did. I wanted to call you and talk, but I was afraid you'd shout at me."

"Shout at you? Whatever for? You're the one who left me." My arms crossed over my chest.

"That's my point." He sighed and ran his fingers through his hair as he pulled off his toque, readjusting a few wayward strands. "I didn't like how we just ended things. How *I* ended things. You were being totally honest, and despite the complete and uncomfortable disclosure, later I had to admit it was refreshing. Never had I been with anyone who hid nothing." He tipped his head to the side and stared up to the roof. "Did that sound right?"

I nodded and understood the point he was trying to make.

"Your relationship with Daniel had nothing to do with me, and yet, you shared it."

"Because I believe honesty is core to a relationship, even if it took me a bit within my own to discover." My smile softened as I sensed the edges of tension between us melting away.

"I agree. But what does this have to do with you showing up tonight?"

"Wait, I'll show you." I ran out to my car and grabbed the accessory off my front seat, placing it firmly on my head. Walking back into the café, I shook my head a little so the bells on the antlers would ring.

"You're too cute."

I twisted my head, jiggling my way back to him, loving the smile creeping across his features.

"I got these for you. The first time I met you, you were wearing them."

"True." His gaze roved above my eyes.

"And that day, you mentioned something about the magic of the season, which is something I haven't been able to get out of my head."

"Go on, I'm listening."

"Your order's ready," the baristo called out to Noel, who walked over and grabbed both our drinks, setting mine in front of me.

Noel sat across from me and wrapped his hands firmly around his drink.

"You know, I've been thinking about how I'm a things-happen-for-a-reason kind of girl, and you're a magic-of-the-season kind of guy, and I think those two things sort of merged over the past week." Where was I going with this? Last night, it had all sounded perfect, but giving a voice to it, now it sounded corny and mildly uninteresting. Somehow, I managed to keep my sigh to myself as I rolled the base of my drink around. "Had I not been, for lack of a better term, banging my boss, he never would've sent me to pick up Bentley that afternoon. I would've never met you and things wouldn't have changed in my life. All that happened for a reason."

"Maybe it was more like the holiday magic's hand in it?"

I shrugged. "Perhaps. But whatever it was, it led me to you. You opened my eyes to a new way of thinking, and you saw me in a way I hadn't seen myself in. All this time, I thought I loved Daniel."

Noel rolled his eyes, but thankfully, he was fairly quick about it.

"But it wasn't love. It was lust. I know in my heart, I wouldn't have been happy with him long term, as you were right, cheaters going to cheat, and I'd be wondering about that the entire time. That's not love. And there was no honesty between us as everything was hidden. From employees, although they knew anyway, from his family. It was all lies."

He shook his head. "Definitely not a romantic love, that's for sure."

"And then you waltzed into my world, or me into yours, as that could be up for debate, and something changed. Maybe it was the antlers you wore, or the way you are with your students, or how you were decidedly honest with me. It was something."

"Magic?" His smirk spread epically from cheek to cheek.

"Could be." I cast my gaze to my drink and wrapped my hands around it. "Whatever it is, I can't get enough of it though. I know I'm being greedy, but I want more."

"Of me?"

"Yes." I locked my gaze onto him, watching as different emotions zipped over his perfectly chiselled jawline with just the right amount of scruff, and eyes that could hold me prisoner for eternity and I've never complain. "Now before you shake your head no and leave, hear me out. This morning I quit my job."

"What?"

"It was… It's… Let's just say, this is best for everyone involved. I no longer have to deal with Daniel, and there won't need to be this awkward working relationship anymore. I have the hard work and dedication to my job, and the credentials to back me in obtaining a new position. Plus, I've already reached out to head-hunters." It had been easier than I thought too. A quick update to my resume, and few clicks, and boom. Done. My inbox already had one request. "But all I wanted for Christmas is you."

"Wanted?"

I loved how he caught the slightest word change. "No, I still want you. If you'll have me, giant flaws and all."

He leaned back in his chair, pushing back so it rocked on two of its legs as his brow furrowed, and a deep, pensive expression settled over him. "You promise to continue being honest with me?"

"I don't believe in lying. Ever." I gripped my cup tighter and stared at the vent in the lid. "There are a million reasons you shouldn't be with me, but maybe there are a million reasons why you should try."

The apples of his cheeks pushed higher with each passing heartbeat. His chair settled back down on all four feet. "Give me two."

"Well, for starters, I'm here right now asking you to forgive me."

Noel's chair scrapped across the floor as he jumped it over to me, searching my eyes and seeing into the depths of my soul. Without another word, he leaned over and kissed me, those sweet lips parting just enough to lead to a promise of more. He pulled away and stared.

"I hadn't given you the other reason yet."

His finger covered my mouth. "You're the first to ever ask for forgiveness so that seals it for me. I'm willing to try if you are."

My vision blurred with his sweet words. "Just like that?"

A smile stretched across his face as he snapped his fingers. "Just like that. I believe in forgiveness. I believe in the magic of the season. And, and this part is really important, I trust my gut. Like I said earlier, when I left the other night, it was wrong. I shouldn't have stormed away, but I needed a chance to think. Surprisingly, I'm not a deep thinker and my only thoughts were of what I'd just walked away from. I feel deep down as if I need to explore this relationship with you. To take you out to more dinners and show you off to the world."

I snuggled closer to him to finish the tantalizing kiss he'd started. "I'd really like that."

"Great! Are you interested in coming to a fun and wildly exciting staff party?"

"If it's on your arm, you bet." My hand cupped his cheek, and I turned his head toward mine. "Merry Christmas, Noel."

"Merry Christmas, Britannia."

With one kiss, Noel had warmed me up and given me hope. I couldn't wait to ring in the new year with him and see where our time together would take us.

Epilogue

One Year Later

I reached under the tree and retrieved the unopened gift I'd been waiting to give him all morning. "Last present coming up."

Noel accepted the light, but sizeable present. "I don't know what else you could possibly give me that you haven't already?" He glanced around. "Having me move into your apartment."

Which was bigger and had a nicer view of the city than his, but he eagerly agreed to sell his.

"Or getting Magick." Our cute tabby cat, who pushed my patience when it came to the

Christmas tree as she would not leave it alone. "Or everything else. This last year has been the best of my life."

"Mine too."

I'd moved on to a better business and was now working for a pharmaceutical company, with its headquarters based a few blocks from my tower. Daniel was still head of Holden Enterprises, but rumour was he was heading for a very costly divorce. Apparently, another assistant he'd been banging wasn't pleased to find out about his marriage and went postal on Mrs. Holden when she showed up unannounced. A staff member got it all on video. Or so I was told from Janice, who accepted my offer to come and join me.

"Do you still believe in Christmas magic?" Noel sat on the edge of the couch.

"Always." I pushed the box in his lap. "Open it."

"Okay, okay, okay." Taunting me, he slowly opened each end and ripped along the folded taped edge, gently lifting the paper.

"You're killing me."

He put the present aside and got on the floor. "Aw, don't die. I want you to live a long and happy healthy life."

"Then open the damn present."

"I will. But first, I want to kiss you, because I haven't kissed you enough today. And I want to thank you for all this magicalness." He pulled me into his lap, and I draped my legs around either side of him. Slowly, he ran his hand up my thigh, over my back and down the length of my arm. "Britannia, I love you so much."

I reached behind him and grabbed the box, putting it between us. "Me too. That's why I want you to open the damn box."

"I will, I promise." Noel held my hand and lifted, staring at it. "Oh no, what happened?"

"I don't know." I flipped it around and checked out the palm, not seeing whatever it was Noel saw.

"Let me see again?" He pulled my hand and checked it out completely, flipping it over and finally settling it on his thigh. "It's missing something."

Before my heart beat again, a gorgeous rose-gold coloured band with a pear-shaped solitaire slipped onto my finger. "Britannia Edwards, will do you do me the honour of marrying me? Some day."

My gaze left the sparkling stone and settled on his face. Expectation hung in the air and it took me a moment to catch my breath as tears rushed to the surface.

"Yes!" The word fell out of me in a rush, and my blurry focus flipped between the ring and his face, unsure of where to land. As my heart picked up speed, it settled on his gorgeous face. "Yes, of course, you can be my husband." A child-like giggle rolled from my lips as I stared into the eyes of the man who held my heart.

He set the unopened gift beside him and pulled me in so close there was no air between us, not that I cared. His kisses rendered me speechless, and the metaphorical ground beneath us always shook with the passion and pleasure he brought into my life on a daily basis.

Gasping for air, but wanting more, I pulled back and smiled into his affectionate eyes.

The twinkle was there in all its glory. "I love you with all my heart and soul."

"I love you too, my darling Noel. You are my breath, my life, and my forever. I can't wait to be married to you."

After a year with a man who lavished attention on me at every moment and never failed to show his affection, it seemed to have rubbed off. A year ago, I wouldn't have been caught dead saying those smooshy sentiments, and now I was spewing as easily as he did. I tugged on the paper of his last unwrapped gift.

"Will you open this now?" I cocked an expectant eyebrow at him.

This time he tore the paper off and lifted the flaps on the box. A smile bigger than anything I'd ever seen cracked his face in half, but he didn't pull the gift out to admire it, setting it down beside him. Rather, his eyes filled with tears. "For real?"

"Merry Christmas."

The End

Dear Reader

Thank you so much for reading my thirteenth published novel (but my nineteenth written.) It was so much fun to write Noel – my first Christmas story, and let me tell you, when it's 30C outside, it's really hard to write. Thank goodness for Christmas music and earphones because that's what got me through!

If you loved Noel, be sure to join my mailing list (link through my website www.hmshander.com) to be kept abreast of all the fun coming out. I promise not to spam you (they come every two weeks) and I include lots of deals and freebies (including a scavenger hunt in the words). Your time is valuable, and I appreciate how you've spent time reading my story (thank you for that!).

As an author, it makes my day when a reader or blogger share their thoughts and gives me feedback on the characters they've invested their time in. When readers fall in love with a character, it's encouraging to write more.

So, if you don't mind, share with me what you liked, what you loved, or even what you hated. I'd love to hear from you via email, my website, or a review on your favourite retailer site. It doesn't have to be long, even just as simple as "Loved this book, looking forward to the next one" works. Reviews and ratings help me gain visibility, and as I'm sure you can tell from my books, reviews are tough to come by. Reviews are like hugs, and I LOVE hugs.

Thank you so much for spending time with me.

Yours,

H.M. Shander

Acknowledgements

NUMBER THIRTEEN! Hopefully, *lucky* number thirteen!

First – my Shander family – Hubs, The Teen, and Little Dude. I am blessed beyond belief to have such an amazing family, who allow me to do what I love, and support and encourage me. Thank you for cheerleading when I'd have a sale or a new release. Thank you for encouraging me to keep going and to chase my dreams, and for the nonstop coffees I sometimes needed when I was on a role. I love you all with my whole heart. It warms my heart to see you writing away on your own stories, to share them with me, and ask for my feedback.

To my parents and in-laws and extended family – Thank you for your support, endless cheerleading, and encouraging your friends and family to give my books a try. Having you visit me at markets and book signings means the world. I have an amazing family, and every day I'm thankful to you all. Thanks for being you.

To my wonderfully dedicated alpha reader – Mandy. Seriously, thank you for being my go-to gal, and reading those raw, unedited chapters after I'd have a couple of rounds at them. You rock at highlighting the great plot points and hitting me between the eyes with the truth about what's not working! I don't know where I'd be without your help.

To my critique partner – Josephine. Thank you for your specialty in helping me stay true to my voice and for your dedication in keeping the characters true to themselves. You deserve a gold star! I'm thrilled that you're now a published author and I'm excited for you to pursue your dream!

To my editor – Irina. Thanks for your quick turnaround time to fixing my errors and highlighting the inconsistencies, and for being able to squeeze in this novella on such short notice when I got approved for the box set with weeks to go until the deadline. I'm so grateful for your word wizardry.

If I missed you, it certainly wasn't intentional. I know I couldn't be where I am without the help of so many others. Thank you! And thank you for reading and making it all the way to the end. You all rock

About the Author

USA TODAY bestselling author H.M. Shander is a star-gazing, romantic at heart who once attended Space Camp and wanted to pilot the space shuttle, not just any STS – specifically Columbia. However, the only shuttle she operates in her real world is the #momtaxi; a reliable SUV that transports her two kids to school and various sporting events. When she's not commandeering Betsy, you can find the elementary school librarian surrounded by classes of children as she reads the best storybooks in multiple voices. After she's tucked her endearing kids into bed and kissed her trophy husband goodnight, she moonlights as a contemporary romance novelist; the writer of sassy heroines and sweet, swoon-worthy heroes who find love in the darkest of places.

If you want to know when her next heart-filled journey is coming out, you can follow her on Twitter(@HM_Shander), Facebook (hmshander), or check out her website at www.hmshander.com.

Manufactured by Amazon.ca
Bolton, ON

36208305R00072